MAISIE HITCHINS

THE CASE OF THE VANISHING EMERALD

Holly Webb

Illustrated by Marion Lindsay

First published in Great Britain in 2013
by Stripes Publishing, an imprint of
Little Tiger Press
This Large Print edition published 2013
by AudioGO Ltd
by arrangement with
Little Tiger Press

ISBN: 978 1471 362019

British Library Cataloguing in Publication Data available

Printed and bound in Great Britain by
TJ International Limited

For Lucy and Madeleine
~HW

For Anna, Fuzz Emily, Nicola and Neil
~ML

31 Albion Street, London

Attic:
Maisie's grandmother and Sally the maid

Third floor:
Miss Lane's rooms

Second floor:
Madame Lorimer's rooms

First floor:
Professor Tobin's rooms

Ground floor:
Entrance hall, sitting room and dining room

Basement:
Maisie's room, kitchen and yard entrance

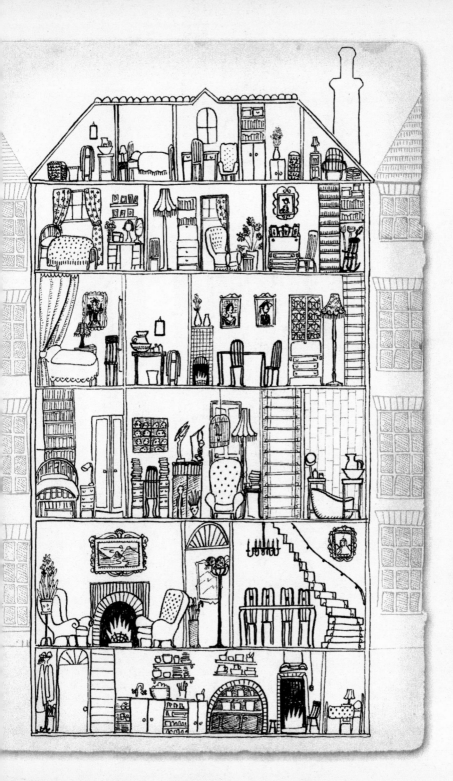

Chapter One

'Maisie! Maisie!'

Maisie Hitchins looked up from the hallway of her gran's boarding house to see Lottie Lane, the actress who rented the third-floor rooms. She was hanging over the banisters in a most undignified way—Gran would have told Maisie off for doing that—but she still looked beautiful, even upside down.

'Yes, Miss Lane?'

'Maisie, can you bring up tea for me and a guest later on, dear? A friend of

1

mine from the theatre is coming to see me.'

Maisie nodded. 'I'll tell Gran,' she said with a sigh, as she flicked her duster over the picture frames. Miss Lane vanished back up to her rooms, and Maisie trailed along the passageway to pass on the message.

'What is it, Maisie?' her grandmother asked, as she came into the kitchen. Gran was sitting at the big wooden table with Sally, the new maid, showing her how to polish silver properly. Gran complained all the time about Sally not knowing which end of a broom was which, but Maisie thought Gran actually quite liked her.

Sally didn't seem to mind her new job, even though it was such a huge change from the butcher's where she used to work. She'd been caught borrowing money from the takings, to pay for her little sister's doctor's bills. Maisie had got to the bottom of the mystery, then got Sally the job with Gran when she had been sacked from the butcher's, so it had turned out all right in the end.

That was what Maisie did best—solving mysteries. She adored puzzles, and was planning to become a detective when she was older. Gran didn't approve of this idea in the slightest, but Maisie thought there was still time for her to come around to it.

Maisie would scour Gran's newspaper every day for mention of her favourite detective, Gilbert Carrington. But Mr Carrington seemed to have disappeared from the papers at the moment.

Maisie's gran peered at her anxiously, and Maisie stood up straighter and tried to smile. If Gran thought she was bored and miserable, she would probably say that Maisie needed to work harder. She would decide to have spring-cleaning early (it was December), and make Maisie take down and wash all the curtains. Or they'd whitewash the kitchen, or some other awful job. Or, even worse, she might decide that Maisie was sickening for something, and she needed a particular disgusting tonic. There was a bottle of cod liver oil at the back of the larder somewhere, and Maisie had no intention of letting Gran dig it out.

'It's Miss Lane, Gran,' Maisie said. 'She says, please can I take up some tea for her and a visitor later on?'

'Oh! I wonder who it is,' said Sally, her eyes shining. 'It could be a famous actress. I saw Miss Lane in *Penny Piece*, she was so lovely. I'd love to go on the stage...'

'You would not, my girl,' Gran said sharply. 'Such nonsense. And the hours that Miss Lane keeps. Never in before midnight! Sleeping till ten! It isn't right.'

'But Gran, the shows don't start till eight! How could she get home any earlier?' Maisie pointed out.

'Humph.' Gran clearly didn't have an answer for that. 'Well, that doesn't explain why her rooms are always such a mess,' she said, with a sniff. 'I hope her friend isn't shocked.'

Maisie giggled. 'Miss Lane might just tidy up a bit. She'll have to, if she wants her friend to be able to sit down.'

'Maisie Hitchins! You're supposed to clean that room. How can you let her get it into such a state?' Gran said crossly.

'It's not my fault!' Maisie protested. 'I have to dust round the mess, Gran! Miss Lane always says not to tidy up or

5

she can never find anything. She made me promise!'

'Ridiculous,' Gran muttered. 'Now, have you finished the dusting?'

Maisie sighed and crouched down to stroke Eddie, her puppy, behind the ears. He had been lurking under the table, in the hope that someone might drop something he could eat.  Sally had dropped a polishing cloth on his head, but that was all, and he looked as depressed as Maisie did. Maisie thought he was missing detecting, too—he was very good at sniffing people out and was as brave as a lion, except when faced with really large alley cats. Maisie called him her faithful assistant. All proper detectives had faithful assistants.

'Yes, I've finished the dusting,' Maisie admitted, expecting Gran to find her another job. She didn't mind helping out with the work in the boarding house, of course she didn't. It was very good of Gran to look after her. Maisie's father was away at sea, and she hadn't seen him for three years, six months and eleven days (she kept a note in a little book that lived under her mattress), so Gran was all Maisie had, as her mother had died when she was a baby. Gran worked hard to make ends meet and Maisie was proud to help her. But over the last couple of weeks, it had felt like work, work, work and nothing else.

Nothing interesting had happened for ages. No mysteries at all. Usually Maisie could at least count on the French lady—Madame Lorimer—who lived on the second floor, to lose her knitting a couple of times a week. Maisie always used her magnifying glass to try to find it. But Madame Lorimer had been confined to bed with a streaming cold and the knitting was in its basket, just where it was supposed to be. And that meant that Maisie's lovely magnifying glass had stayed uselessly in the pocket of her petticoat, except when she took it out to polish.

Gran looked at Maisie with her head on one side. 'Well, perhaps you could go to the grocer's and fetch me a pennyworth of liquorice,' she said thoughtfully.

Maisie stared at her. Gran hated liquorice, so it must be a treat for her!

Gran reached over to find her purse and handed Maisie the penny with a little smile. 'Go on then, and take the dog,' she said, nodding. 'Oh, and don't eat all of the disgusting stuff on the way home, Maisie, or you'll be sick. Make it last.'

Maisie hugged her. She hadn't had any money to spend on sweets for ages. The house at 31 Albion Street brought in good money from the lodgers, but times were hard. Maisie knew that Gran was worrying about the leak in the roof, and how she was going to find the money to get it mended. Gran had a bucket in her room collecting the drips, and Sally said it was coming through her side of the attic now, too. She'd had to move her bed to stop it dripping on to her nose.

'Are you sure?' Maisie whispered, and Gran smiled.

'A penny won't matter, Maisie. You're a good girl, you deserve a treat.'

'Thanks, Gran!' And Maisie hurried away to find her jacket before she could change her mind.

That afternoon, Maisie toiled up the stairs with the heavy tea tray. Even though Gran said she disapproved of theatre people, she clearly wanted to impress Miss Lane's guest. Maisie was carrying the best china and the silver-plated teapot that had been one of Gran's wedding presents. She was curious to see the actress who had come to visit—Sally had opened the door to her and said that she was very smartly dressed, and had a beautiful hat, but she couldn't see what the lady looked like, as the hat had a veil.

Maisie knocked on Miss Lane's door with her elbow. There was a scuffling

noise, and a piteous wail and Maisie heard Miss Lane murmuring something. She stared at the door in surprise, wondering if she ought to go away and come back with the tea later. But then the door opened and Miss Lane peered out at her, looking harassed.

'What is it? Oh, Maisie! I'd forgotten the tea.' She turned back to speak to the lady who was sitting in the armchair by the fire. 'Sarah, dear, do try to cheer up. Maisie's brought us some sustenance. You'll feel better after a cup of tea, won't you.'

Sarah? So that was the actress's name. *Sarah who?* Maisie wondered. Perhaps she was famous.

'She's upset,' Miss Lane told Maisie, quite unnecessarily, as Maisie could see past Miss Lane to the armchair and the litter of damp handkerchiefs around it.

'I'll bring the tray back down later, Maisie,' Miss Lane sighed. '*Much* later, probably...'

Maisie was quite reluctant to go downstairs. She wanted to see what was going on, but she couldn't think of any excuse. She was just being nosy, she thought to herself, sighing. But it was because she was naturally nosy that she was such a good detective!

It was a good two hours later, while Maisie was peeling potatoes for supper, that she heard the front door bang. It must be Miss Lane's guest leaving.

'Go and fetch that tray, Maisie,' Gran said, turning round from the stove. 'I'll want it to send up Professor Tobin's supper.'

Professor Tobin had the first-floor rooms, and he was Maisie's favourite lodger. His rooms were full of stuffed animals in glass cases and strange weapons and masks, and things that Maisie simply had no idea about at all. They were a nightmare to dust, especially the glass cases, but Maisie forgave him for that, because he would talk to her while she cleaned them, telling her stories about his travels. He had been *everywhere*, as far as Maisie could tell.

When Maisie came up the stairs to Miss Lane's room, the door was slightly open and she could see Miss Lane collapsed in an armchair, looking exhausted. She waved vaguely at Maisie to come in.

'Are you all right, Miss Lane?' Maisie asked worriedly, as she tidied the teacups back on to the tray.

'Yes. But I'm worn out, Maisie. Actresses are just so—tiring! Sarah

13

would not stop!'

'Is she a *very* famous actress, Miss?' Maisie asked curiously. 'As famous as you?' she added, to be tactful. Miss Lane was always in work, but she wasn't really a household name.

Miss Lane chuckled. 'You're very sweet, Maisie. That was Sarah Massey and she's, hmmm, *almost* famous. If you haven't heard of her by now, you almost certainly will do soon. She's playing at the Dauntry Theatre at the moment, and she'll be a household name one of these days.' She sighed. 'Well, she will if we ever sort this nightmare out, anyway…'

'Why, what's the matter with her, Miss? Is it her young man?' Maisie asked sympathetically. Miss Lane had complained to her in the past about the various young men that hung around the stage door and got under their feet.

'Yes,' said Miss Lane. 'Oh, he hasn't been cruel to her, though, Maisie. Quite the opposite, actually. He wants to marry her.'

'Marry her?' Maisie frowned. 'But that's good, isn't it, Miss?'

14

'Oh yes, and she wants to marry him as well,' said Miss Lane. 'Which is even better, but it's the necklace, you see. That's what's causing all the trouble.' Miss Lane frowned at Maisie. 'Oh, I shall have to tell you the whole story. But you mustn't breathe a word. It's the deepest, darkest secret. Promise you'll keep it to yourself.'

Maisie's eyes glowed. She sat down on the hearthrug next to the tea tray and stared up at Miss Lane eagerly.

'A few months ago, Sarah told me that a young man started coming to see the show night after night. He always sat in the front row, in the middle seat if he could get it. And he would spend the whole evening gazing at Sarah. He sent flowers to her. He left chocolates for her at the stage door. It went on for weeks, until at last he sent her a note with the chocolates, asking if he could perhaps take her out for afternoon tea—her and a friend, as he wanted to be very proper.' Miss Lane smiled. 'He was so polite, Maisie, and by this time she was so curious about him that she said yes, and you can guess who that friend was.'

Maisie nodded and Miss Lane smiled at her. 'She asked me to go with her. He met us at the ABC Tea shop, and he bought us buns.' Miss Lane sighed. 'And that was that. They've been smitten with each other ever since, Sarah and Mr Timmy Fane.'

'But if he wants to marry her...' Maisie said, frowning, 'I don't see why she's unhappy. It all sounds perfect.'

Miss Lane nodded. 'It does, doesn't

16

it. Except Mr Timmy Fane *isn't* Mr Timmy Fane at all. He's a lord, Maisie. The son of a duke, and his name's Tarquin. He's only just told her. And honestly, what sort of a name is Tarquin to saddle a poor child with?'

'But that's even better,' said Maisie. 'Doesn't she want to marry the son of a duke?' Maisie began nibbling one of the biscuits Gran had sent up with the tea. Miss Lane and Miss Massey hadn't touched them, which just showed how upset they were.

'Of course she does! She'll be a duchess then—well, one of these days!' Miss Lane rolled her eyes. 'Sarah, a duchess...' she said faintly. 'I can't imagine it...'

Maisie shook her head. 'So, I still don't understand why she's upset.' As far as she could see, marrying a duke sounded wonderful. She was willing to bet duchesses never had to do dusting, and they were probably allowed to do a bit of detecting in their spare time as well! 'Oh!' Maisie had a sudden thought. 'Does he want her to stop being an actress?' she added, frowning.

'No, it's not that,' said Miss Lane. 'Quite the opposite. In fact, he says he loves it that she's so clever. No, the problem is that Timmy gave Sarah a necklace. Very pretty, nice pearl beads, and a big green glass pendant with little sparklies all round it. He said it matched her eyes—you wouldn't have been able to tell that this afternoon, she'd been crying so much, but Sarah's got lovely green eyes.' Miss Lane frowned. 'Well, anyway. She loved it. Wore it all the time, until a couple of days ago, when it disappeared. She left it in her dressing room while she was on stage, and when she came back, it had gone.'

Maisie gasped. 'Gone?' That was terrible! But then she had another thought. 'If he's so rich, can't he buy her another one? I know it's sad, but couldn't she just explain what happened?' Maisie asked.

Miss Lane shook her head. 'It's not as simple as that, Maisie. You see, when Timmy told her he was really Tarquin, he told her about the necklace too. They were real pearls,

Maisie. A string of matched freshwater pearls, and the sparklies were diamonds, and that green glass pendant?' Miss Lane leaned forward and whispered dramatically. 'An emerald, Maisie! One of the biggest emeralds in the world! We'd never even dreamed that it might be real—it's as long as my thumb, for goodness' sake.' Miss Lane stared gloomily at the glowing ashes of the fire. 'It's an heirloom. Worth thousands and thousands of pounds. Every Fane bride wears it on her wedding day. Tarquin clearly wanted Sarah to have it, but the idiot didn't think of telling her until much later how precious it was until a couple of days ago! Now how can she tell him she's lost it?'

Maisie nodded slowly. She could see why Miss Massey had been so upset.

'Maybe you can find it for her, Maisie,' Miss Lane sighed. 'You're really good at mysteries.' But Maisie could tell that she didn't really mean it.

'I'll take the tray down now, Miss, if you don't mind,' she said, getting up, and Miss Lane nodded.

Maisie went slowly down the stairs, balancing the heavy tray and trying to think of ways she might find a jewel worth a king's ransom. It would be so good to have a proper mystery to solve!

But she'd never even been to the Dauntry Theatre, where Miss Massey was appearing. Maisie had never been to *any* theatre! Gran didn't approve of them. How could she investigate if she couldn't even imagine the scene of the crime?

'Miss Maisie!'

Maisie was so deep in thoughts of priceless emeralds that Professor Tobin's whisper took her completely by surprise. She jumped and nearly dropped the tea tray, sending Gran's best sugar bowl sliding dangerously towards the stairs.

Professor Tobin caught it, and stared at her apologetically. 'Sorry, Maisie. I just wanted to ask you...' He looked around rather guiltily and then leaned close to whisper—so close Maisie could see the tufts of hair growing out of his ears, and the biscuit crumbs on his bowtie. 'Was that Miss Sarah Massey I saw going up the stairs earlier?'

'Yes,' Maisie said, staring at him in surprise. 'Do you know her, Professor?'

'Oh no!' Professor Tobin shook his head. 'No, not at all. But I've seen

21

her—she's playing the lead role in *Circus Sweethearts*, you know. I've seen it four times. She's a wonder! Her voice! Her dancing!'

'I didn't know you liked the theatre, Professor,' Maisie said, trying not to giggle. She couldn't imagine the professor watching a musical show.

'It is the greatest of the arts, Maisie, quite the greatest...' Professor Tobin suddenly frowned at her worriedly. 'But Miss Massey seemed to be upset. Is something wrong?' He breathed in, puffing out his chest, and Maisie realized that he was imagining himself rescuing the lovely young actress from a fate worse than death.

Maisie frowned. She probably ought not to tell him. But if the professor knew the theatre, perhaps he would be able to help her investigate. He might be able to suggest a way Maisie could get into the theatre.

'It's a secret,' she began doubtfully. 'You must absolutely promise not to tell...'

The professor nodded eagerly.

'Miss Massey is going to be married

to a duke—well, almost a duke. He will
be one day. And he's given her a
beautiful emerald necklace, but it's
been stolen, and she doesn't know how
to tell him. It's worth thousands and
thousands of pounds. I was thinking, I
could try and help her look for it...'
Maisie added shyly. 'But really she
ought to tell the police. She doesn't
want to, though, because then they'd
be bound to tell Lord Tarquin Fane, as

the necklace really belongs to him. She hasn't told him yet as she's worried he'll be furious with her. Perhaps she could ask the famous detective, Gilbert Carrington, to help,' Maisie said dreamily. 'Except I think he must be out of the country at the moment.'

'Lord Tarquin Fane? You mean the Marquess of Fane?' Professor Tobin's bushy eyebrows shot up. 'An emerald? Goodness, Maisie, did he give the girl the Stone of Saint Cecilia?'

'I don't know.' Maisie looked puzzled. 'It was a necklace, with pearls, and an emerald pendant.' Maisie stared at him. 'Miss Lane said it was as big as her thumb. Could that be the Stone of Saint Cecilia? The emerald's got a name?'

Professor Tobin pulled at his moustache, trying to remember. 'Let me see... The Stone of Saint Cecilia. Mmm... One of the most famous jewels in the world. It was found in India, yes, hundreds of years ago, and for a long time it was in a church of Saint Cecilia in Italy—in the crown of a statue of the saint, I seem to recall. But

24

the church was destroyed by an earthquake and the stone was stolen. Eventually it came into the hands of the Fane family, in about 1700. Since then it's been one of their greatest treasures. They put it in a necklace. There are legends about it.' The professor frowned. 'It was thought that the stone had actually been stolen from Saint Cecilia's statue before the earthquake, and that was why the church collapsed. All nonsense, of course.'

Professor Tobin pulled out an enormous spotty handkerchief and wiped his forehead. 'But it's one of those jewels that gathers dark stories about it. Legends of ruin and disaster for its owners, if it should be lost. The family are all supposed to die of a terrible wasting sickness, if I remember rightly. Poor girl—when she finds out about the curse, she'll probably think she's brought it down on herself and Lord Tarquin.'

'Do you think maybe Lord Tarquin won't marry her if she can't find it?' Maisie asked worriedly.

Professor Tobin sighed. 'Considering she's just lost approximately a third of his fortune, I should think he might possibly have doubts...'

Chapter Three

'Hello, Maisie! Oi, don't let that dog
near the sausages...' It was the next day
and Maisie had just run into George—
the delivery boy from the butcher's.
George held the parcel with the meat
delivery up over his head and
pretended to glare at Eddie, who was
dancing round his feet and yapping
excitedly.

'Don't tease him,' Maisie said,
giggling. 'You make him worse. He
wouldn't dream of even *looking* at a

sausage if you didn't encourage him. How's work?'

George shrugged. 'All right, I suppose. The new girl that took Sally's place—she's the most stuck-up thing you've ever seen. She acts like she's too good to work in a butcher's shop, she's

enough to make a cat laugh. You ought to see her waltzing around with her nose in the air. She says I smell, Maisie, can you imagine? She's got a lacy handkerchief with lavender water on it, and she holds it up to her nose when I go past.'

Maisie shook her head disgustedly. George *did* smell of the shop, she had to admit, but that was hardly a surprise, and the shopgirl probably smelled of sausages and the best mince, too.

'Hey, Maisie,' George added, as he passed her the meat order. 'Isn't that Miss Lane who lives upstairs friendly with Miss Sarah Massey? The one who plays Lily in *Circus Sweethearts*?'

Maisie groaned. Had everyone heard of the actress except her? 'Yes. Why? What of it?' she asked.

'Well,' said George. 'Miss Massey didn't go on last night. She's had an accident. It's in all the papers and the newsboy was shouting about it.'

'What sort of accident?' Maisie asked worriedly. 'Is she all right? Was she badly hurt?'

George shrugged. 'Don't know.

Anyway, I thought your Miss Lane might want to go and visit her, or something.'

Maisie nodded. 'It's kind of you.' She knew quite well that George just enjoyed passing on gossip, but then Maisie did like to gossip, too, so she could hardly tell him off. 'I'll take Miss Lane's letters upstairs and tell her the news,' she promised him. 'So have you seen her play?'

'Course I have!' George said. 'Everyone's seen it, Maisie, it's the talk of London. I've seen it twice. I got a seat up at the back. It's fantastical.' He gave her a surprised, rather pitying look. 'Haven't you seen it, then?'

'No...' Maisie muttered, going pink. 'Gran isn't keen on the theatre. She thinks it's not proper. All that dressing up and glittery stockings...'

'Your gran's just fussy,' George said, rolling his eyes.

By the time Maisie had put the meat away in the larder, the front door was banging closed and she realized crossly that Miss Lane had gone out—and now someone else was bound to tell her about Sarah Massey's accident. Maisie would just have to try to catch Miss Lane later, and hope she would feel like gossiping. Maisie sighed sadly, and got on with the washing-up.

A little while after their midday dinner, Maisie heard Miss Lane coming back and talking to Sally in the hallway. She hurriedly filled the kettle and put it on the stove. It was almost tea time, if one liked tea early, anyway. And Miss Lane often didn't eat dinner if she was busy, so it would be a kindness to take her a cup of tea...

Maisie assembled it on a tray and shut Eddie in the kitchen so that he didn't trip her up on the stairs—he never meant to, but he was only a puppy and he had a habit of weaving in and out of feet.

Then she carried the tray up to Miss Lane's room, and knocked hopefully.

'Oh, Maisie, you little treasure,' Miss

Lane murmured, as she flung open the door. 'I need that tea. I've spent the whole morning fussing over Sarah at her lodgings, and if you think I'm untidy, Maisie, you should see what she's like. And her landlady isn't nearly as nice as your gran. I haven't had so much as a biscuit.'

'George told me Miss Massey had had an accident...' Maisie prompted, hopefully.

'Oh, yes, she had the most lucky escape, though. She was crossing the road, and she was nearly run down by a hansom cab. The cabbie said she wasn't looking, but Sarah swears she was.' Miss Lane frowned. 'Though she's so featherbrained at the moment, Maisie, I should think it probably *was* her fault. Since Tarquin told her about the emerald being valuable, she just hasn't been thinking straight, and now she's learnt about some sort of curse on the stone, although that's all just superstition.'

Maisie frowned. 'I thought she was a star, Miss Lane. How can she get away with being featherbrained? With all those words to say, and the dancing, and the songs?'

'Exactly,' Miss Lane said grimly. 'It's that dratted boy Timmy's fault. Well, Tarquin. Sarah's been in such a tizzy she can hardly remember if she's coming or going. Even before the accident, I think the manager of the theatre was getting tetchy. It's up to him who gets the starring roles, you see, and until a few days ago, he thought Sarah was wonderful. Pretty, and she's got a lovely voice, and charm, Maisie. That's what made her so special. You could feel her smile all the way to the back row of the gods—that's the bit right up at the top, dear.'

Maisie sighed. She wished Gran wasn't so strict. Even the butcher's boy knew more about the theatre than she did.

'But she's still got all that,' Maisie pointed out.

Miss Lane shook her head. 'She's distracted, though. Forgetting her lines, messing up the steps in the big chorus dance number. Oh, they covered for her, but the audience could see it wasn't right. And the charm's gone, Maisie. The sparkle. She's too worried to shine.' Miss Lane sighed. 'It's even worse now, of course. She's convinced it's all because of the curse, especially since she was nearly run over by that dratted cab. Have you heard about this curse, Maisie?'

'Professor Tobin told me about it,' Maisie nodded. 'About it being bad luck to lose the emerald.'

'Yes,' Miss Lane said grimly. 'So now, of course, Sarah thinks she's probably going to die some sort of horrible lingering death.'

'So has Lord Tarquin noticed that she's not wearing the necklace yet?' Maisie asked.

'She had enough sense left to tell him that the clasp was loose, and that she had taken it to the jeweller's to be mended,' Miss Lane explained. 'But I think that used up the last of her wits. Now she's just a jittery mess.'

'So, what happened last night? Did they have to cancel the show?' Maisie asked anxiously.

'Oh no,' Miss Lane shook her head

briskly. 'No, her understudy went on instead—one of the chorus girls, who knows the role in case Sarah's ill.' Miss Lane wrinkled her nose worriedly. 'And unfortunately for Sarah, she was very good. Arabella's a dear girl, very sweet and sensible. She was in the chorus in the last show I did at the Gadsby. I wouldn't be surprised if she was as well known as Sarah, one of these days. The theatre manager practically kissed her after the curtain calls, so one of my other friends told me. Sarah's been so worried about Timmy and the necklace, she hasn't exactly made herself popular. Too many leading-lady temper tantrums—someone moved the parasol she uses in one of the dances, and then the ribbons on her shoe broke, and she made a bit of a fuss about it. And now Arabella's there, just as pretty and no trouble at all, and she knows the part backwards...' Miss Lane sighed. 'I tried to warn Sarah, but she screeched at me! And then she apologized, and then she cried. A lot. May I have another cup of tea, Maisie?'

36

'So you think Miss Massey might lose her part?' Maisie breathed. It was fascinating.

Miss Lane nodded slowly. 'I think she might—if she doesn't start making more of an effort to keep it, anyway.'

Chapter Four

'Maisie! Maisie! Are you there?'

Maisie, Gran and Sally all looked up in surprise.

'Is that Miss Lane calling for you?' Gran asked, looking anxious. 'You did do out her room nicely this morning, didn't you, Maisie?'

'I did,' said Maisie. 'And I lifted up all the piles of clothes and books and things, and I put them back exactly the same afterwards.'

'And you didn't break anything?'

'Of course not!' Maisie rolled her eyes.

Miss Lane suddenly appeared at the kitchen door in her smart outdoor coat and a beautiful velvet hat. 'Oh, my goodness, it's freezing out there,' she said, brushing at her sleeves. 'It's even beginning to snow.'

'Is there anything you need, Miss?' Gran asked, standing up.

'Oh no, no... Well, actually... It isn't anything to do with the lodgings, Mrs Hitchins, don't worry. Everything's perfect. But I wanted to ask you something, you and Maisie.' Miss Lane looked at her hopefully. 'Could I sit down for a minute and talk with you?'

Gran nodded doubtfully and then glared at Sally. 'Put the kettle on, girl! And Maisie, you fetch that seed cake out of the larder.' Gran bustled about, clearing the vegetables off the table, and dusting a chair for Miss Lane with her apron. The lodgings at 31 Albion Street were quite smart, and lodgers did not usually turn up in the kitchen. It made Gran jumpy. But now Miss Lane was here, she had to be treated properly.

'What can we do for you, Miss?' Gran asked once Miss Lane was seated with the best silver-plated teapot in between them, and the seed cake on a glass dish. Maisie sat next to Gran, with Eddie at her feet, who was hoping for cake crumbs.

'I need help, Mrs Hitchins. To be quite straight about it, I need Maisie.'

Maisie nearly dropped her teacup, she was so surprised. 'What for?' she gasped excitedly.

'Mind my best china, Maisie,' Gran snapped. 'What do you mean, Miss Lane? What do you need Maisie for?'

'Has Maisie told you about my friend, Miss Sarah Massey? She's appearing at the Dauntry Theatre. She's the star.'

Gran looked slightly uncomfortable. 'I'm afraid I don't know much about the theatre, Miss. I'm too busy for gallivanting about.'

Miss Lane nodded. 'Of course. But Miss Massey is very nice. A very sweet girl. The thing is, she's been terribly unlucky recently. A necklace was stolen, a valuable one, and actresses are very superstitious, you know.' Miss Lane smiled. 'I never, ever let a black cat cross my path, Mrs Hitchins. I'd be convinced that something awful would happen.'

'Lot of nonsense,' Gran muttered, but not very loudly. Maisie knew for a fact that Gran felt the same way, and she always looked at her tea leaves after she'd finished the cup.

'Some silly person told Sarah that the necklace was cursed, and she'd brought disaster on herself by losing it. So now, of course, she's *so* worried that everything seems to be going wrong.'

'Poor dear,' Gran said sympathetically.

'Yes,' Miss Lane agreed. 'But I don't think it's anything to do with a curse. I think someone—someone very unpleasant—could be playing tricks. Playing on Sarah's nerves. Trying to make her lose the star part.'

'But that would be so cruel!' Sally gasped.

Even Gran clicked her tongue disapprovingly. 'Poor child.'

'Do you think Miss Massey would stop worrying about all her bad luck if she got the necklace back?' Maisie asked.

Miss Lane sighed. 'Well, probably. But I don't see how she will. Sarah made such a fuss when the necklace disappeared that all the cast and the stage crew are being searched before they leave each night, which makes me think that whoever stole it must have hidden it in the theatre.'

'Unless, of course, the thief got it out of the theatre before she even noticed it was missing,' said Maisie.

'That's true,' said Miss Lane. 'But it

43

seems unlikely—they would have had to be very quick about it.' Miss Lane was quiet for a moment, as if she was thinking it through. Then she sighed. 'Anyway, they can't keep the searching going on for much longer. Sarah says that everyone's been complaining about it. And if they stop, sooner or later someone will be able to sneak it out. And to be honest, they could have done already if they were daring.' She winked at Maisie. 'I bet I could hide an emerald pendant somewhere in my petticoats.'

Gran sniffed disapprovingly, and Miss Lane tried to look serious. 'Well, on the positive side, there are a lot of people around the theatre at the moment, in and out of each other's dressing rooms all the time, so it would take a lot of nerve to try and sneak it away.'

'Do you have any idea who could have stolen it?' Maisie asked, pulling out her little notebook from the pocket of her apron.

Miss Lane sighed, and shook her head. 'No. Not a clue. And I've an awful feeling we never will.'

Maisie frowned and nibbled on her pencil. 'Wait a minute. You said everyone thought the necklace wasn't valuable, didn't you? Or not very valuable, anyway. You thought it was glass. So why would anyone want to steal it?'

'Oh!' Miss Lane looked surprised. 'You're right. I hadn't thought of that...'

Maisie leaned forward, frowning. 'Isn't it a bit strange that all these horrible things are happening to Miss Massey now, just after the necklace was stolen? Just in time to make her think that the curse is working... Could anyone at the theatre have known what the necklace really was? Even Miss Massey didn't know.'

Miss Lane nodded. 'That's true... So someone must have worked out what it was before ... before Sarah even knew herself!'

'But perhaps it wasn't stolen so that the thief could sell it. Or that wasn't the main reason, anyway, given all these latest events,' Maisie murmured.

'Because someone who works in a theatre isn't likely to know how to sell a fabulous emerald, are they? You couldn't just take it to any old jeweller's shop. They'd need a—a criminal mastermind.' She nodded to herself, proudly remembering the phrase from Gran's newspaper. 'I think it must have been someone who doesn't like Sarah. They stole the necklace just so they could make her think she was cursed!'

Miss Lane looked at Maisie in surprise. 'I hadn't even thought of that, Maisie. Goodness, I can see why you're so good at this detecting business. But how would they have known who Timmy was, and what it was he'd given her? Even Sarah didn't know for ages.'

Maisie frowned thoughtfully. 'I'm not sure about that bit.' She turned to Gran. 'Miss Massey's admirer is the son of a duke,' she explained. 'He didn't tell her who he was to begin with—but there are drawings of people like that in the society pages of the papers, aren't there? Photographs, even, sometimes. I know Miss Massey didn't know who he was, but maybe someone else recognized him?'

Slowly, Miss Lane nodded. 'I think that could be it, you know. And they might have been jealous... Sarah's only nineteen. That's very young to have such a starring part, and there's been a lot of horrible, catty talk from the girls in the chorus. Lots of them think it should have been them playing the part. If someone found out that Sarah had a lord as an admirer, as well... And she kept on showing off that pretty necklace.' Miss Lane laughed. 'Even I got a little sick of Sarah telling me how beautiful her necklace was, and I'm her friend!'

'So they might decide to steal it, just to serve her right?' Maisie suggested.

'Exactly... Oh dear, it's even worse than I thought,' Miss Lane murmured. 'Mrs Hitchins, please do say I can borrow Maisie.'

Gran stared at her. 'But you've still not said what you want her for, Miss Lane!'

'Oh!' Miss Lane shook her head. 'Sorry. It's spending the morning with

Sarah—I'm all mixed up. She needs a dresser. Someone to help her in and out of her costumes, and tidy her dressing room, that sort of thing. And with the way things are at the moment, it needs to be someone that Sarah can trust. Someone who knows what's going on with Tarquin, and won't gossip! I told Sarah she could certainly trust Maisie.'

'But what's happened to Miss Massey's own dresser?' Maisie asked, feeling excited. She'd wanted to go to the theatre, just to see a show. She'd never, ever thought of working in one.

'That's the thing. Lucy's broken her leg,' Miss Lane said grimly. 'She fell down the stairs.'

'Someone pushed her?' Gran asked, her voice full of horror.

'No. It was cleverer than that, Mrs Hitchins. Pushing her would be too obvious. The stairs were greased. Only a little, but it was enough, if you were running down them in high-heeled dancing slippers.' Miss Lane pressed her cheeks with her hands wearily. 'Lucy only came down the stairs

49

because Sarah had forgotten her fan, you see. She had to run back and fetch it. Otherwise, the next person down those steps would have been Sarah, all in a hurry as she had a quick change before her next entrance. It was meant to be Sarah that fell, not poor Lucy.'

'No!' Sally gasped.

'I think so.' Miss Lane nodded. 'I can't prove it, of course. No one thought to check the stairs at the time. But Lucy's up and down those stairs ten times a day. And she said she didn't trip—her feet just sort of slid out from under her. That made me think.'

'And you want my Maisie to go and work in this place!' Gran said, her voice full of disapproval.

'Oh, Gran, please!' Maisie stood up.

'I want someone Sarah can trust, Mrs Hitchins. A good, well-brought-up girl who can help her in her time of trouble.'

'Hmmm...' Gran still looked doubtful, but Maisie could tell she was softening. She'd always tried her best to bring Maisie up nicely.

Suddenly, Maisie remembered that

Miss Lane was an actress, too. Not quite as much of a star as Miss Sarah, but still a very clever actress. It was the way she leaned over and fixed Gran with her dark blue eyes, and her voice went a little bit husky and slow. Gran stared back at her like a confused rabbit. 'It's her duty, Mrs Hitchins,' she said. 'Maisie is so clever, and she notices things. If whoever it is tries to play any more tricks on Sarah, she'll spot it. And she might even find that dratted necklace.'

'Well, I suppose she might be able to...'

'And,' Miss Lane leaned even closer, 'she'll be very well paid. Don't tell me that a little extra money wouldn't come in handy, Mrs Hitchins. I heard you talking to that man about the leak in the roof.'

'I'd do my work here before I went to the theatre, Gran,' Maisie promised, staring at her hopefully. 'I wouldn't leave it all to you and Sally.'

Gran sighed. 'I suppose so. But don't you go getting ideas, Maisie Hitchins. You're only helping out. Just for a week or two!'

Chapter Five

Maisie glanced at the young girl in the plain green dress and then looked round at Miss Lane, who was following her into the dressing room. They had been told that Sarah Massey was here, but she didn't seem to be. The girl was the only person in the room.

But Miss Lane hurried into the room and hugged the girl tightly. 'Sarah! Darling, are you all right?'

'I suppose so,' she answered, sullenly.

Maisie blinked. This was the famous Miss Sarah Massey? She looked about seventeen—younger than Sally. She certainly didn't look old enough to be playing the main role in a play. And surely actresses wore silk dresses, and velvet capes, and furs? Miss Lane would never wear such a plain gown!

The girl had been staring dolefully into the mirror in front of her, but now she turned to look at Miss Lane.

'Nothing else has happened, has it?' Miss Lane asked anxiously.

'No,' the girl sighed. 'Except that the theatre manager came in to show me this.' She held up a newspaper, folded down to show a marked page. Miss Lane took it and started to read.

'Sources in the theatre world have told us... Young, flighty actresses... Unreliable! Waste of money on expensive tickets...

Oh, it's just some silly gossip column, Sarah. What are you reading nonsense like that for?' Miss Lane closed the paper and flung it into the corner of the room, but Maisie noticed that she looked worried.

'The manager says it's about me. He says everyone in London knows that I'm demanding and horrible, and now I'm ruining the show!' She gulped and her shoulders shook.

Maisie passed Miss Lane a clean handkerchief, and Miss Massey looked up and saw for the first time that she was there.

'Oh! Is this the girl, Lottie?'

'Yes, this is Maisie. I've borrowed her from my landlady, just for a few weeks. And I've explained what's been going on. Maisie won't breathe a word, will you?'

Maisie shook her head hurriedly. 'Oh, no!' she whispered. She was a little daunted by the hugeness of the theatre. The backstage area where they were now seemed to be a rabbit warren of passages and little rooms and more passages, and a lot of dust, but Miss Lane had shown her the front of it, too. The theatre was all built in white stone, with gilded statues, and huge posters with drawings of the stars, and extracts from the newspaper reviews. One of them had said that Miss Massey was 'a glittering comet sparkling across the heavens'. Maisie found it hard to imagine—Sarah Massey didn't look the least bit glittery just now. She looked plain and tired, and her nose was bright pink.

'Thank you,' Miss Massey sniffed, and managed a small smile at Maisie. When she smiled it was just about possible to see her as a famous actress, but even so... 'Can you stay tonight?' Miss Massey asked. 'I've been borrowing one of the girls who helps in the wardrobe, but the others need her, and they've been complaining again. I can understand why,' she added, sighing.

'I can stay,' Maisie agreed. 'I'll stay now, shall I? And clean up for you.' The dressing room was dusty, and there were clothes hanging over chairs, and a vase of fading flowers on the long dressing table in front of the mirror. There were even a few mouse droppings in the corner of the room. But even if it hadn't been grubby and untidy, Maisie would have made some sort of excuse to stay. There was a sense of excitement running through the dusty corridors, even now, hours before the show was due to start. And she felt sorry for Miss Sarah—she was so young, and she looked so miserable.

'Wonderful!' Miss Lane agreed. 'I have to go—I have a rehearsal—but I'll leave you with Sarah. Maisie—you know your way home, don't you? I'll tell your gran you'll be back later on.'

Maisie nodded and stared a little anxiously after Miss Lane as she whisked away. She did know the way back, but she wasn't used to being out so late. In fact, she was a little worried that she might fall asleep in the middle of her work, and then have to walk back later through the noisy streets...

Miss Sarah smiled at her again, a proper smile this time. 'I'll get the doorkeeper to fetch you a cab. I can pay for it, Maisie, don't worry. I'm very glad you've come. Lottie said she wasn't sure she could get you, but if she did, you'd be the answer to all my prayers.'

Maisie went pink. 'I'll do my best, Miss,' she said. But inside she was deciding that she had to solve this mystery. She must. It was a real case—she'd been hired to be a dresser, but Miss Lane wanted her to be a detective, too. She was almost a professional!

'That's it. No, even tighter, Maisie.'

Maisie yanked on the ribbons and gasped. 'Honestly, Miss Sarah, how can you sing with your corset this tight? You can't even breathe! It's making me out of breath and I'm not even wearing it!'

Miss Sarah giggled. 'You get used to it. And the dresses wouldn't fit if I left it any looser.'

Maisie tied the ribbons, and went over to fetch Miss Sarah's dress for the opening number.

'I hope you don't mind me asking, Miss...' she murmured. 'Miss Lane told me about Lord Tarquin and everything.'

Sarah nodded. 'I know. She said you thought you might be able to help me find the necklace. That you're good at that sort of thing.' Her face clouded. 'But I don't think anyone will find it now, Maisie, it's been missing for more than a week. I'm sure it's been stolen.' Sarah sighed miserably. 'I made a huge fuss about it—that's partly why everyone's so cross with me. I threw a proper screaming fit. I don't know what came over me. I loved that necklace, before I knew what it was. It made me think of Timmy whenever I wore it.' She gave a little laugh, remembering. 'I said I'd walk out if it wasn't found. I can't believe I was such a shrew. I made them search everyone's dressing room, and the stage doorkeeper still has orders to search everyone's pockets before they leave.'

Maisie couldn't believe it, either. Miss Sarah was so lovely. 'So the necklace really must still be in the theatre!' Maisie said hopefully.

Sarah shook her head. 'I thought so at first, but a necklace isn't all that big. Someone could have smuggled it out— hidden in their washing, or something like that. I can't see old Mr Jones on the door getting all the chorus girls to shake out their skirts, can you?'

'No... I suppose not,' Maisie agreed. 'But Miss Sarah, what about Lord Tarquin? Does he still think it's at the mender's?'

'He's gone to visit his father.' Sarah gulped and pressed her hands against

61

her heart, as though it was fluttering with panic inside her. 'He's gone to tell him about me. That he wants us to get married. His father's bound to be dreadfully shocked. Actresses aren't the sort of person that a duke usually marries.' Her voice rose to a wail again. 'And then next week, when he gets back, I shall have to tell him the truth about the necklace and he won't want to marry me any more, anyway!'

Maisie patted her hand sympathetically. 'You never know. We might still find the necklace before then.' But she couldn't feel very hopeful. As Sarah said—the necklace was probably long gone.

'Sarah! Have you heard?' A very pretty girl a little older than Miss Sarah was peering round the door, her face worried.

'No... What is it, Arabella?'

Maisie watched anxiously as the colour drained out of Miss Sarah's face, leaving her yellowish white, her hands gripping the back of the chair so tightly the bones showed.

'What's happened?' she whispered,

her eyes huge, and darker green than ever.

The girl by the door looked uncomfortable. 'I'm sorry, I shouldn't have sprung it on you like that. I just saw it, and—'

'What?' Sarah almost screamed it, she was so wound up, and suddenly Maisie could understand the stories Miss Lane had told her about the actress's tantrums. She was scared, all the time. No wonder she lost her temper.

'Someone's thrown red paint all over the posters at the front,' Arabella said quietly. 'And broken the glass. It's just about everywhere.'

'Oh...' Sarah said quietly, sinking down into the chair. 'Just my ones, I suppose?' she added in a bitter little voice. 'My reviews are smashed? And my picture?'

'Yes,' Arabella admitted, looking down at her hands. 'I shouldn't have said...'

'I had to find out some time.' Sarah buried her face in her hands. 'They'll sack me. I know they will,' she gasped.

'The publicity. It'll be in the papers. It's the necklace. That's what it is,' Sarah choked out. 'I'm cursed. It won't stop! Not till I'm dead, probably!'

Maisie stood watching worriedly, wondering if she should comfort Miss Sarah, but Arabella had already hurried in and was kneeling by her chair. 'Of course they won't! The theatre manager wouldn't be so stupid. You carry this show, you know you do.' Arabella hugged her. 'It's that horrible old stone,' she said. 'It has to be.' And when she caught Maisie's eye in the mirror, she looked scared. 'I've got to go, Sarah, I need to get changed and do my hair.'

A moment later, she stood up and patted Sarah's shoulder awkwardly. 'It'll be all right, I'm sure it will.'

'So you've told her about the necklace, too?' Maisie asked thoughtfully, as she closed the dressing-room door.

Sarah sniffed, and nodded. 'A lot of people know now. Rumours fly round here. But I told Arabella myself. She found me crying, after Timmy had told

me about the necklace, and who he really was. I had to explain. Arabella was lovely about it—so excited for me. She said she was sure I'd find it again soon, and we agreed that the curse was only a silly story. It couldn't be true. But then after that all the awful things started to happen, and it is true! It is!'

Maisie looked at her with concern. She really did seem to believe she was cursed, and Arabella had believed it as well. Maisie didn't believe in curses. But both of the older girls had looked terrified.

'I don't think a necklace could break glass, Miss,' Maisie said matter-of-factly. 'Even if it is cursed. Or throw red paint everywhere. I don't think this is a curse at all. Of course, it's a real pity about the necklace, and we'll have to do our best to find it. But all the accidents, and Lucy falling down the stairs—that's real. It isn't a ghost, or bad luck or fate. You've got someone trying to scare you silly. We just need to find out who. And you've got me to help you...'

Chapter Six

A little later, whilst the play went on, Maisie slipped out of Sarah's dressing room and into the chorus girls' room. There was something burning in the stove. She walked over and opened it. Grabbing a singed piece of fabric from inside, she tucked it inside a handkerchief and stuffed it into her apron. Then she clanged the door shut, wincing as her fingers burned on the hot metal. She whisked out of the dressing room, ducking quickly behind a clothes rail that was standing in the passage. She could hear running feet pattering on the stairs and someone was laughing. Maisie held her breath, shaking her sore fingers as the chorus girls poured past her into their dressing room, ripping off their feathered headdresses, ready for the next change.

As soon as they were all inside, Maisie darted back into Sarah's dressing room along the passage.

'Maisie, where have you been?' Sarah said, looking round at her anxiously. 'I need you to help me put the finale dress on. Oh, my goodness, what have you done to your hands? You're covered in black stuff! Don't come near my dress like that!'

'I won't, I won't. I'll wash them. I'm sorry, Miss Sarah.' Maisie hurriedly washed the ashy streaks off her hands in the bowl of hot water she'd brought in for Sarah earlier on.

Sarah sighed. 'You look like you've been grubbing about in a fireplace or something.'

Maisie smiled at her. 'I was in the chorus girls' dressing room, Miss. I wanted to look round while there wasn't anyone there, you see, while they were all on stage, and the dressers had gone to get a cup of tea. I didn't want anyone knowing that I was snooping about, that way they won't know to mind their tongues while I'm around.' She pulled the little bundle out of her pocket, wrapped in her shamefully grubby handkerchief. 'Look, Miss. Don't come close enough

70

to mark your dress, though.'

Sarah peered over at the scraps of burned fabric and wrinkled her nose disgustedly. 'Whatever is it, Maisie?'

'It's a pair of gloves, Miss. What's left of them.' She twitched at the fabric and held it up closer. 'Can you see the red paint?'

'The posters!' Sarah gasped.

'Mm-hm. I found them in that big old stove in the chorus girls' dressing room. Whoever did it wore gloves, and then they burned the evidence in the stove. Or tried to. I took them out of the back of it.' She smiled at Sarah. 'Do you still think it's a curse, Miss?'

Sarah nibbled her bottom lip, staring at the stained gloves, as though she'd never seen anything like them. 'Maybe not,' she admitted. 'Perhaps you're right and someone is trying to scare me.' Her face seemed to lighten as she smiled and the worried lines along her forehead smoothed out a little. 'I suppose whoever it was knew how much theatre people believe in things like that.'

Maisie nodded. 'It has to be

71

someone from the theatre, Miss. *This* theatre. If it wasn't, they could have just thrown the paint around and run away—there would be no need to come inside. This is definitely someone who you know. They belong here.' She placed the handkerchief-wrapped bundle carefully on one of the shelves and started to help Sarah into the huge, flouncy dress. 'There has to be someone here who doesn't like you very much, Miss.'

Sarah laughed sadly. 'That doesn't narrow it down a lot, Maisie. I got picked out of the chorus a year or so ago to take a part in *Mermaid Girl*, and that led to this show afterwards. A lot of the girls thought it should have been them that got chosen.I hoped they'd come round to the idea, but they still hate me for it. And people like Edward Hart and Millie Morrison, who have the other main parts, they think I'm just a jumped-up chorus girl who got lucky, so they can't stand me, either!'

Maisie sighed. 'Well, at least it's not a curse, Miss. If it's just some spiteful

dancer, we've got a chance of stopping them, haven't we?' She looked thoughtfully at Sarah in the mirror, as she began to do up the line of tiny buttons. 'I might go visiting the chorus dressing room again, Miss. When they're there, this time.' Her smile widened. 'And if I moan a bit about how mean you are, Miss, and how you threw a bottle of scent at me, maybe they'll tell me things.'

'I did not!' Sarah gasped. 'Oh—oh, I see, Maisie. I'm being stupid. You're very good at this, you know. But not scent. No one would believe that, it's too expensive. Face powder, maybe.'

'It looks as though you *have* been throwing the face powder around,' Maisie said sternly, looking at the dressing table. 'It's everywhere, Miss.'

'I'm sorry, Maisie.' Sarah frowned. 'I'll try to keep it tidier. I can't think how it got like that. I'm sure I didn't spill it.' She undid the pretty glass jar, and lifted out the powder puff, fluffing it into the loose powder, ready to dab it over her face before she went back on stage.

Maisie watched her, gazing thoughtfully at the drifts of powder scattered over the bench, then she let out a little squeak of dismay and snatched the powder puff, just as Sarah peered into the mirror and held it up to her face. 'Don't!'

'What is it?' Sarah stared at her.

'If you didn't spill that powder, and I haven't touched it, then someone else must have been at it, Miss!'

Sarah looked at the little jar in horror. 'You think they could have done something to it?' she whispered.

'Very possibly.' Maisie dusted the powder puff lightly across the back of her hand, and then grimaced. 'Itching powder. Someone mixed itching powder into the jar, Miss,' she said, holding out her hand. Tiny little red bubbles were already appearing on her skin.

'Maisie! Wash it off!' Sarah shrieked. 'Quickly, before it gets worse!' She seized a cloth and started wiping the powder away. 'If I'd put this on my face,' she murmured. 'I can't even imagine… I have to go, I'm on in a minute.' She hugged Maisie tightly. 'Lottie told me you'd be worth your weight in gold, and you are.' She shook her head, smiling. 'You're a proper little detective, aren't you. Do you know, I almost believe you might even find that necklace for me.'

It was very nice that Sarah believed in her, Maisie thought, as the cab rattled home through the dark streets. But how on earth was she going to find the necklace? It was likely that Sarah was right, and that it had been spirited away from the theatre long ago. But then, when the necklace was stolen, not even Sarah had known how valuable it was. Whoever had taken the jewel might well have done it to upset her, and not for its value. That would mean that there was still just a chance that it had been hidden somewhere in the theatre.

Unfortunately, though, the theatre was so full of holes and corners and possible hiding places that Maisie had no idea where to start.

The cab drew up at Albion Street, and Maisie thanked the driver, stifling her yawns, and hurried round to the back entrance through the yard. She was planning to creep in quietly and go straight to bed—it was almost midnight—but there was a light burning in the kitchen.

'Gran! You waited up for me!'

'I didn't have much choice, Maisie. That dog of yours has been fussing as though he thought you were never coming back.'

Eddie was running round and round Maisie's feet, jumping up and down and yapping and squeaking with excitement.

'Oh, Eddie! I'm sorry. Did you miss me?' Maisie picked him up, laughing, and he squirmed around in her arms so that he could lick her nose.

'Barking and whining... I've never heard him like that, Maisie. I don't suppose you can take a dog with you to that place?' Gran asked pleadingly.

Maisie frowned. 'Actually... They do have a terrible problem with mice. Miss Sarah told me one of her costumes was nibbled all round the hem once. And they've got traps everywhere, but I still saw a mouse in Miss Sarah's dressing room.' She nodded thoughtfully. 'I could set him to guard the dressing room, too. Someone played a horrible trick on Miss Sarah today, messing with her make-up. They couldn't have done that if Eddie had been there. I'm sorry he kept you up, Gran.'

'Oh well...' Gran smiled into her sewing. 'I might have waited up for you, anyway, Maisie.'

Chapter Seven

The next evening, Maisie was back at the theatre.

'And what do you want?'

Maisie ducked her head and tried to look shy and downtrodden as the tall girl with the shiny, dark hair stared at her snootily.

'Who are you, anyway?' Another of the chorus girls turned round and stared at her, and Maisie wondered if her cloud of reddish curls were dyed. *They looked it*, she thought cattily.

Gran would have been shocked.

Lil, one of the dressers, who helped the girls in and out of their complicated costumes, turned round to look. 'Oh, it's just Maisie. She's Miss Massey's new dresser. Standing in for poor Lucy.'

'Ugh...' The red-haired girl shuddered. 'I don't even want to think about that. Those stairs are a deathtrap. The management should do something about them, they really should. We're up and down them so many times, it's a wonder we haven't all broken something.'

Maisie considered saying that she thought the steps might have been greased, so she could see if anyone looked guilty, but decided against it. She didn't know the chorus girls well enough yet—the only one she recognized was Arabella, fiddling with her hair over on the far side of the room. It was hard to tell if someone felt guilty if you didn't know what they *usually* looked like.

'I don't know,' Maisie murmured shyly. 'Seems to me Lucy might be glad of the rest.'

The dark-haired girl stared at her. 'What do you mean? She broke her leg!'

Maisie gave a little shrug. 'But now she's got at least a couple of weeks laid up and Miss Massey's still paying her.' She shuddered dramatically. 'She's probably thanking her lucky stars. I've only been here a day and I could do with a week's holiday already.'

'That bad, is she?' the red-haired girl

laughed and looked properly at Maisie for the first time. 'What did she do?' she asked, glancing slyly sideways at the others.

The dark-haired girl stopped tying the ribbons on her shoes and stared at Maisie eagerly. 'What's she been saying to you?' she asked, giggling. 'Did she accuse you of stealing her jewellery? She's going to get the police in to search us all for her stupid necklace, I suppose!'

'Flora! Kitty!' Arabella turned round and glared at the girls. 'Why do you both have to be so mean? Sarah hasn't done anything to either of you. And *someone* must have stolen that necklace.'

'Oh, *Sarah*, is it? Friends with her, are you?' the red-haired girl, Flora, snorted in disgust. 'She's a stuck-up little witch and she doesn't deserve that part.' She reached over and put an arm round Maisie's shoulders. 'Tell us all the gossip, sweetheart. Is she a monster to work for?'

Maisie sniffed sadly and crossed her fingers in the folds of her skirt. 'She slapped me,' she whimpered. 'And she threw a jar of face powder at my head! It only just missed me.'

'I thought so! You see, Arabella! Your darling Sarah's got a nasty temper.' Flora nodded triumphantly.

Arabella shrugged and stared at Maisie. 'Well, I don't believe it. And I don't think you should be spreading tales about her if you want to keep your job.' She went and stood by Maisie and Flora. She caught Maisie's chin between her fingers and pulled her head up, so she could look into her eyes.

Maisie stared back at her defiantly, scowling. She didn't much like Arabella. Whatever Miss Sarah said, there was something a little too sweet about her face. Syrupy, almost...

She was obviously a real friend to Sarah, though. It would have been really easy to keep quiet while Flora and the dark-haired Kitty made their horrible comments. They were just jealous of Sarah's good luck.

But were they jealous enough to steal the necklace? She could imagine them playing nasty, mean little tricks— she wouldn't be surprised if they did that sort of thing to each other all the time—but the necklace was a little bit different.

Maisie glanced at the clock on the wall and gasped. 'I'd better get back, or Miss Sarah'll have the skin off me.'

Kitty laughed. 'Good luck, Maisie. Remember to duck if she picks up the face powder again!'

Maisie smiled and waved as she ran out of the dressing room, but as soon as she was in the passageway a frown crept across her brow. She had a couple of suspects—Kitty and Flora. She ought to have been feeling pleased with herself, but something was niggling at her. It didn't seem quite right.

Chapter Eight

Maisie struggled out of bed the next morning at her usual time to do her cleaning, but Gran sent her straight back again. 'You can do your housework later on,' she said firmly. 'You need rest. You're already earning your keep, Maisie. I might not like the thought of you at that theatre, but I can't deny they're paying you well. And it was nice of Miss Sarah to send you home in a cab. Considerate.'

Maisie went back to bed with Eddie

curled luxuriously on her feet, but she found it hard to sleep, even though she was tired. She was worrying about the necklace—and how she could work out who it was playing the mean tricks at the theatre. Perhaps she could set some sort of trap to see if she could catch one of the girls in the act?

Miss Sarah didn't quite believe in the curse any more, so the pranks weren't scaring her in the same way, but they were still dangerous. Poor Lucy was still laid up at home. Miss Sarah had said that she was going to visit her today, and take her some nice food.

Maisie yawned and turned over, squeezing her eyes tight shut. She had to sleep—she was still weary after her second late night, and she had to do it all over again later on. As she fell asleep, sparkling emeralds seemed to dance in front of her eyes, just as she imagined the chorus girls did at the theatre.

Later that afternoon, Maisie set off for the Dauntry Theatre, with Eddie trotting happily beside her. She was glad to be taking the little dog with her—she had missed him, even with all the excitement of the theatre. But she walked a little slower as she came up the alley to the stage door, hoping that she wouldn't get shouted at by the doorkeeper for trying to bring a dog inside.

Mr Jones the doorkeeper did peer out of his little booth in surprise, but he seemed to like dogs, and he smiled down at Eddie. 'He's a fine little lad, isn't he.'

'He's very good at catching mice,' Maisie explained. (It was quite true. Eddie lined them up outside the back door and dragged Maisie out to admire his haul every so often. It annoyed him that she cleared them away.) 'Miss Sarah said there were a lot of mice around, so I offered to bring him.'

'Good idea,' nodded Mr Jones. 'Send him down this way, Maisie—the little blighters are always after my sandwiches.'

Maisie hurried in, hoping that Sarah would approve of her idea, too. It helped that, by pure luck, Eddie happened to dive under the costume rack that was still standing in the passage and came out with a limp, furry little mouse in his jaws, just as Sarah hurried down the passage.

'Oh! Is he yours, Maisie? He's so sweet. What a clever little dog!'

'Yes, Miss. I thought he'd be a help with the mice.' Maisie leaned over and added, in a whisper, 'And he can guard the dressing room, Miss, if we need him to.'

'Yes, of course! That would be good. Mr Lorenzo—he plans the dances, you see—he's made a change in one of the scenes. So now I'll need you in the wings to help me take off that awful hat as well, and give me the parasol for the

91

Sunny Days number.' Sarah smiled. 'It'll mean you can watch some of the show, Maisie. Would you like that?'

Maisie beamed at her. So far, all she knew about the show was that it was set around a circus and that lots of the musical numbers involved juggling, and even a high-wire that was stretched across the back of the stage. She would love to see what all the backstage work was actually for.

She waited eagerly for the second half of the show, when Sarah would need her to be on the side of the stage. As they left the dressing room at the

end of the interval, Maisie settled Eddie on an old blanket in the corner of the room and they hurried away.

Maisie hadn't known what to expect of the theatre—she had peeped in at the rows and rows of dusty-looking velvet seats and been rather disappointed. It was almost shabby. But now, watching from the wings as the chorus rushed on for the big dance number that opened the second act, Maisie found it hard to catch her breath. The stage glittered with light and there were pale watching faces stretching away into the darkness for

miles. Here and there the stage lights picked out a gilded statue at the side of one of the boxes. It was like a palace. Or as close as Maisie had ever been to one.

It was wonderful to feel that she belonged here, just a little—more than the people out on the other side of the lights did, anyway. She watched delightedly as the dancers milled across the stage in delicate, shifting patterns, with Sarah twirling in the midst of all of them. Maisie had never seen her dance before, of course, but to her, Sarah seemed perfect. Surely no one could think she wasn't up to the part any more.

There was a huge surging wave of applause and even cheers as Sarah ran off hand in hand with Mr Edward Hart, who played her suitor. He smiled at Sarah approvingly as Maisie started to unpin her hat.

'Good show tonight,' he said, nodding, and Sarah stared at him for a second in surprise, and then smiled.

'You're bringing me luck, Maisie,'

she whispered, as he strode away. 'He never says anything nice normally.'

Sarah had to be on stage again in minutes, with her hair loose, and a frilled parasol to twirl in the dance. Maisie was looking forward to this bit. Sarah had described it to her—how she had to walk about the stage as if she was in a daze, while the circus performers rehearsed around her. She had to walk in an exact pattern, she'd explained, or the jugglers would hit her.

Maisie watched, holding her breath, as the balls flew backwards and forwards, arching over Sarah's head as she went on dreamily twirling her parasol. It was very pretty, and funny, too, and she could hear the audience laughing.

They laughed even more when a small white and brown dog appeared at the edge of the stage, athletically leaping up to catch one of the balls in his teeth. It looked just like part of the act, but it wasn't...

'Eddie!' Maisie gulped from the wings, and she tried to beckon her dog off the stage. But she couldn't call him, of course, and he didn't pay any attention. He just sat there with the ball between his paws, looking pleased with himself and letting everyone dance around him.

'I'll be sacked,' Maisie muttered to herself miserably. 'I will be, for sure. Oh, Eddie, come here!'

Perhaps it was because she was crouching down, trying to call Eddie back, but Maisie was the only one who saw what happened next. It was so quick that she almost didn't see it at all. It was just the tiniest glimpse as Sarah whirled past the little cluster of chorus girls who were pretending to sew sequins on to circus costumes. Just the smallest sighting of pink ballet slipper, as one of the girls stuck her foot out. It could almost have been an accident, but as she saw Sarah trip, and hop, and twirl her way cleverly back into the proper steps, Maisie was almost certain that it had been done on purpose. Not only that, but she'd seen who the pink ballet slipper belonged to. It was Arabella!

Arabella, Sarah's friend, had deliberately tried to trip her up!

'But she's so nice,' Maisie said, shaking her head as she sat with her friend, Alice, back at Albion Street the next day. 'She's the only one who is. Some of the others mutter horrible things about Miss Sarah behind her back, but Arabella stuck up for her. She told me off, when I was trying to stir up gossip! It can't be her. She was the one who came to tell Sarah about the posters, she was worried about her.' Maisie frowned. 'I must have imagined it. Perhaps Sarah tripped after all.'

'Sometimes people aren't always what they seem, Maisie,' said Alice, as she glanced carefully through the banisters to make sure no one was coming.

Maisie was supposed to be sweeping the landing and Alice had escaped from her French conversation lesson with Madame Lorimer. The French lady had a terrible habit of falling asleep in the afternoons, which Alice and Maisie found very useful.

'Just keep an eye out for Miss Sidebotham,' Alice murmured. 'It would be so like her to come back and fetch me early, just when we're getting to the interesting bit. I wish I was too old for a governess.'

'It really can't have been Arabella. She's too sweet to do something like that—but then again, I did see it...' Maisie nibbled her thumbnail anxiously.

Alice rolled her eyes. 'Maisie, for goodness' sake! Arabella's an actress! And she must be a good one, if they're thinking of giving her Sarah Massey's role. Just because she looks sweet and sounds sweet, it certainly doesn't mean she really is!'

Maisie stared at her. 'I never thought of it like that,' she admitted. 'So ... you think it could be an act?'

'Of course it could be!' Alice said triumphantly. 'And she didn't *have* to tell Miss Sarah about the posters, did she? They could have been cleaned up and Miss Sarah would never have known.'

Maisie nodded, thinking it through. 'Maybe she was throwing people off the scent by being so nice about Miss

Sarah... Perhaps it's been her all along,' she murmured. 'All the horrible tricks.'

'You'd better keep an eye on that Arabella,' Alice agreed. 'So what happened about Eddie? Did you get into trouble for bringing him?'

Maisie shook her head. 'I thought I would. I was sure they'd get rid of me. But Miss Sarah told the theatre manager that we'd definitely shut the dressing-room door, and that the only way he could have got out was if someone had gone in there, which is true. And no one should have done, of course. So then everybody started fussing about who it was who went in, and they forgot about Eddie going on stage.' She giggled. 'Except that Mr Lorenzo asked me if I thought he could be trained to do it again. I said he could try, but Eddie isn't very good at doing things when you want him to. And now he has to be tied up if we leave him in the dressing room, poor Eddie. Still, it's better than leaving him here to annoy Gran.'

'Ssshhh! That's Miss Sidebotham. Goodbye, Maisie! I wish I had French more often. Do you think you'll have solved it by next week?' Alice slipped back into Madame Lorimer's room, waving to Maisie.

Now that Alice had given her the idea, Maisie did her best to watch Arabella as much as she could. But it seemed that she was a much better actress than anyone had suspected. She was always, *always* nice.

So nice that it was quite suspicious, actually, Maisie decided, after a couple more evenings watching her at the theatre. Surely nobody could be so sweet-natured absolutely *all* the time?

Maisie watched Arabella thoughtfully as she gossiped to Sarah in the dressing room. She did seem to know an awful lot of stories about smart society people—perhaps she *had* recognized plain old Timmy as Lord Tarquin Fane.

Maisie was tidying Miss Sarah's make-up, checking it as carefully as she could. Only last night, she had put away all the sticks of greasepaint, and felt something scratch her fingers. It had taken her ages to work out what it was, and then she had felt sick with disgust. Someone had pushed a hat pin up under the foil cover of the greasepaint stick, so that as it wore

102

down, Sarah would eventually draw a great scratch down her face. It made Maisie even more determined to find out who was playing these horrible tricks. Maisie didn't quite know what she would do when she found out who it was, but she was considering punching them on the nose.

Could it really be Arabella? Maisie would need proof.

Maisie drifted closer to Sarah and Arabella, with the open jar of face powder in her hand (Sarah had sent her out to buy a new jar, after they had discovered the itching powder). As Arabella waved her hand to demonstrate just how ridiculously large a hat the lady in the front row had worn the night before, Maisie squeaked and tipped the powder all down Arabella's dress.

'Oh! You stupid little brat!' Arabella screamed, aiming a slap at Maisie. Maisie dodged so she mostly missed her. Then she ran to the corner and pretended to cry.

Arabella snarled something furious and began to dust frantically at the

dress—it was a beautiful navy-blue velvet, and it was going to be a beast to clean. But Maisie didn't feel all that sorry.

'Arabella, it wasn't Maisie's fault, you knocked the powder!' Sarah said, looking surprised.

'Oh...' Arabella seemed to suddenly remember her sweetness. 'Sorry, Maisie. I shouldn't have lost my temper. This is my favourite dress, that's all. But it really doesn't matter,' she added, smiling, but with gritted teeth.

Maisie sniffed and smiled back, but she had to bite her lip to stop herself laughing. So Arabella wasn't so nice after all. Maisie was beginning to think she would really rather enjoy proving her guilty.

Chapter Nine

'Maisie! Can you take these in to Miss Massey for me?' Mr Jones leaned out of his cubbyhole by the door, waving a pretty little basket of white flowers. 'Hello, sonny,' he added, patting Eddie on the head. 'Heard about your stage debut the other night. Going to take it up as a profession, are we?'

Maisie looked down at Eddie and shook her head. 'I don't think so, Mr Jones. He is very clever, but he's not always clever when he's supposed to be, if you see what I mean.'

Maisie hurried on down the passage to the dressing rooms, clutching the little basket of flowers, and met Sarah just taking off her coat.

'Mr Jones sent these up, Miss,' she said, putting the flowers on the dressing table, next to a huge bouquet of roses that Lord Tarquin had sent from his country house a couple of days before.

'Oh, they're very pretty,' Sarah said, leaning over to smell them. 'What sort of flowers are they? I don't recognize them. Ugh!' She reeled back, holding up the back of her hand to her mouth in disgust.

'What is it?' Maisie cried anxiously.

'Oh, they smell *horrible*,' Sarah said, coughing a little. 'Like onions, or something. Disgusting. Take them out, Maisie, please.'

Maisie picked up the little basket, and sniffed cautiously at the starry white flowers, and the broad leaves. She hadn't looked at them very closely—she'd thought they were Lily of the Valley, or something like that.

But now she could see that they were quite different, and they did smell odd. Very like onions.

'What a foul thing to do,' Sarah muttered, and Maisie could see that her eyes were filled with tears. 'I thought those mean tricks had stopped. Someone must really hate me!'

'I'll get rid of them right now, Miss,' Maisie promised, feeling glad that she hadn't told Miss Sarah about the pin in

the greasepaint. She hurried back down to the stage door, with Eddie scurrying behind her.

'Mr Jones, I don't suppose you remember who brought these?' she asked hopefully, showing them to him.

Mr Jones frowned. 'Isn't there a card? It was just a boy. Not long ago. Just before you arrived. He said a girl had given him twopence to bring them.'

'A girl?' Maisie looked thoughtful. 'So, there wasn't a card.' Maisie shook her head. 'And they're not proper flowers, you know. They smell bad.'

Mr Jones sniffed the flowers suspiciously, and snorted. 'Wild garlic, that is, Maisie! Ramsons, they call it, too. Now why didn't I spot that!'

'The pretty basket?' Maisie suggested. 'It looks like a nice present, doesn't it? So where would you get wild garlic from?'

Mr Jones shrugged. 'Anywhere. It's a weed. Somewhere shady under a tree, maybe? But it would have to have been very sheltered,' he added, frowning again. 'It's proper late for it to be flowering now. Or early, maybe. It's a spring plant. Unless someone took it into a nice warm house and brought them on. Mmmmm. Someone's been planning this a while, I'd say.'

Maisie scowled. She bet she knew who. But she couldn't prove it. Unless—if it was Arabella, wouldn't she want to see how her horrible trick had worked out? She hadn't been able to resist telling Sarah about the posters being splashed all over with paint. She was bound to be hanging around the dressing rooms, waiting for Sarah to burst out crying…

Maisie thanked Mr Jones and raced back up the passageway, peeping into dressing rooms as she went, wondering where Arabella was.

She found her at last in the main chorus girls' dressing room—where the stove was. Arabella had a big bowl of hot water, and she was scrubbing her hands hard, going at her nails with a brush, and sniffing them every so often.

'This stuff stinks…' Maisie heard her mutter, as she sniffed and rinsed again. Then she dried her hands carefully on

110

a towel, and tipped the bowl of water down a grating in the corner. Maisie darted behind a dressmaker's dummy that was standing by the door, pulling Eddie with her, and praying that he wouldn't make a noise as Arabella hurried past. The girl's skirts brushed past her, and even now Maisie could catch a faint whiff of garlic. Arabella

stopped and turned, and Maisie froze, thinking that she'd sensed someone watching her. But instead, Arabella glanced towards the door before she picked up a scent spray that stood on one of the mirrored benches. She sprayed herself generously, aiming the scent at her hands, and wincing. She had scrubbed so hard they looked raw, and the perfume must have stung.

It served her right, Maisie thought. She was sure now that Arabella was playing all the tricks—she must be so jealous of Miss Sarah—but that didn't get her any closer to finding the necklace.

When she got back to Sarah's dressing room, Maisie found her with her face in her hands, her shoulders shaking as she cried.

'What is it? What's happened?' Maisie begged. She shouldn't have been so long watching Arabella.

112

'It's not another horrible trick,' Sarah told her wearily. 'It's Timmy. Lord Tarquin, I mean. It's a note from him. He's back, Maisie. He says he can't wait to see me, but he doesn't want to disturb me before the show. He wants to take me out for a late supper.

113

Oh, Maisie, he'll expect me to be wearing the necklace! Whatever am I going to tell him? I can't pretend any more! He'll be so upset, so angry. He'll break the engagement, I know he will!'

Maisie swallowed anxiously. She thought she knew who the thief was. But she only had a few more hours to find the necklace—before it was too late.

Chapter Ten

At last Sarah dried her eyes, and she gave a little sigh, and a sniff. 'Oh, well. There's nothing I can do, is there? That necklace is probably in the window of a pawn shop somewhere by now. That's the awful thing—whoever took it probably had no idea what it was. They'll have thought it was glass, like I did, and sold it for a few shillings.' She shook her head at Maisie. 'I know it sounds silly, but I wish it had been glass all along.

115

It would have been a lot less trouble.'

Maisie nodded. 'It would, Miss. But Lord Tarquin only gave it to you because he loves you. He wouldn't have wanted you to just have glass. He didn't know how much trouble the emerald would cause.'

'Oh, don't make me cry again!' Sarah wailed. She sniffed, and dabbed at her eyes, and then stared at Eddie, who was crouched down next to the door, running his nose along the floorboards. 'What is he doing, Maisie?'

'I think he's probably smelled another mouse, Miss,' Maisie said. 'I'll let him out, shall I? He won't stop that sniffing and scratching until he's caught it.'

Sarah nodded, and Maisie opened the door, watching Eddie race out into the passage so fast that his paws skidded on the boards. 'I'll just go and check he isn't chasing that mouse anywhere he shouldn't,' Maisie added worriedly. She wasn't sure Eddie would be allowed back in the theatre if he caused any more trouble.

All Maisie could see was a glimpse of white tail, disappearing round the corner, and she hared off up the passageway, just in time to see Eddie bolting into the workroom, where the wardrobe mistress did the alterations, and the new costumes were made. It was lined with cupboards where old costumes were stored in cloth bags until they were needed for another show.

Eddie was skittering backwards and forwards in front of one of the cupboards, growling, and occasionally letting out sharp little barks.

'Oh dear... Did the mouse get in the cupboard?' Maisie asked him, hurrying over, and glancing round for the wardrobe mistress. She didn't think the old lady would want a dog in her workroom. But then she probably wouldn't want a mouse in there with all the precious costumes, either.

'It'll be locked, Eddie,' Maisie tried to tell him. 'Come on... Leave the mouse. I bet Miss Sarah's got a biscuit for you in her bag. Biscuit! Come on, Eddie!'

But Eddie could still smell mouse, and he couldn't chase biscuits. Furiously he sprang up at the cupboard door, battering at it with his little paws. Then he jumped back with a yelp of surprise as it swung open, revealing shelves lined with boots and dancing slippers, and bags and head dresses, all stored in bags and boxes.

Maisie giggled. 'Wasn't that what you wanted it to do? Oh, Eddie, no!'

The mouse was in the cupboard, so Eddie saw no reason why he shouldn't be, too. He took a running leap and sprang on to the first shelf, dislodging a whole row of shoes, and a scruffy-looking wooden box, which hit the floor with a thump.

Eddie snapped triumphantly, and bounced out of the cupboard to lay the mouse at Maisie's feet but Maisie wasn't interested in the mouse—she was staring at the mess in horror.

'Eddie! You monster! I have to clear this up or Annie will kill me!' Annie was the wardrobe mistress, and she'd already told Maisie to be sure not to let Eddie get muddy pawprints on any of Sarah's dresses. She didn't like dogs.

The wooden box was full of sparkly paste and glass jewellery, the kind of thing that looked wonderful on stage from a distance, but didn't look like real diamonds and rubies and sapphires close up. Maisie sighed as she started to scoop it all back into the box. She held the glittering piles up in her hands, letting them run through her fingers. They were so pretty, even if they were fake. This one, for instance. She picked up a beautiful pearl necklace—this must be very like the one that Sarah had lost. The pearls were huge, bigger than peas, and they had a soft glow to them, as though a little light shone inside each one. At the end of the pearl string was a huge emerald pendant that burned and flashed as Maisie swung it to and fro. *It does look ever so real*, Maisie thought. And then she dropped the necklace as if it really had burned her. What were the chances of the theatre wardrobe having a necklace exactly like the stolen Stone of Saint Cecilia?

Maisie picked it up, cradling the emerald in her hands, and then squeaked as Eddie gave it an interested lick. 'You mustn't! Eddie, I think this is it! I think we've found it! This is the real necklace! Someone must have taken it and hidden it in here when they weren't able to smuggle it out. It's the best place to hide anything—in amongst things that look the same. Whoever took it must have hidden it

here until the fuss had died down—
which it hasn't yet, of course.'

Maisie stood up and slipped the
heavy handful into the pocket of her
little apron. Then she quickly picked
up the shoes and boots that Eddie had
knocked down and put them back in
the cupboard. She went to pick up the
jewellery box last of all, but just as she
was sliding it back on to the shelf, she
paused, staring thoughtfully at it.

It was all very well having found the necklace, but wouldn't it be even better to know for certain who had taken it? And she thought she knew just how to prove it. Maisie smiled to herself and took the wooden box with her.

'What on earth are you doing with that?' Sarah asked, staring at the box in surprise. 'I don't need any more jewellery on stage.' Then she smiled sadly. 'Oh, Maisie. Were you thinking that I could find something in here to deceive Timmy? It wouldn't work. The emerald isn't like anything you'd find in a costume store. But you're a darling to think of it. Anyway, I need to tell him the truth. I should have done to start with.'

Maisie had slipped the emerald necklace back into the jewellery box, and now she was setting it down on the bench in front of the mirror and opening it up. 'Are you sure you won't find anything like it in here?' she asked slyly, smiling up at Sarah.

'No, really, you see it's absolutely unmistakable. I can't believe how I was silly enough to think it was glass and

fish-scale pearls in the first place...
Maisie!'

Sarah dropped the greasepaint stick she was blending on the back of her hand and it rolled under the chair, forgotten.

'Maisie Hitchins! Where did you get that?'

'Out of the paste jewellery box, Miss,' Maisie told her, smiling. It was fun to tease Sarah a little bit.

'You found it! You found it! You actually did! Oh, Maisie, just in time!

You little angel! How did you do it?'

'It was Eddie, really,' Maisie explained. 'And the mouse. It ran into the cupboard, and Eddie scrabbled it open and tipped out the box and all sorts of other things. It was only when I was putting the jewellery away that I saw it—just like Miss Lottie described it to me.'

'I can't believe it...' Sarah stroked the pearls wonderingly. 'It was there all the time? Do you think it got there by mistake?'

'No,' said Maisie seriously. 'I'm pretty sure that it's just been hidden there for the time being, ready to take away when everyone's given up hope of finding it.'

Sarah nodded. 'Of course. That's quite clever. Hiding it in plain sight.'

'Miss Sarah ... I've been thinking about how we could catch whoever's been doing all this,' Maisie said, dropping her voice to a whisper.

Sarah stared at her. 'Do you know who it is?'

Maisie chewed her bottom lip. 'I think I do,' she said slowly. 'But unless

I've got proof, you aren't ever going to believe me.'

'I will!' Sarah cried. 'I promise I will, I mean, you've found the necklace. I have to trust you now.'

Maisie took a deep breath. Dare she tell her? 'Well…' she started. 'Well, I think it's Arabella.' Maisie looked at Sarah with her head on one side.

'Arabella?' Sarah frowned. 'But why? Arabella's my friend. She's always so nice to me. Much nicer than the others.'

'I know.' Maisie nodded. 'And that's what put me off the scent at first. I'm not certain, but she gave the game away when she tried to trip you up, once. I saw it. And then when I spilled that powder on her, she was furious. Why would she have been so cross unless she had done something to the powder?'

'You mean she put the itching powder in the jar, too? And she thought it was still there?' Sarah asked, her eyes widening.

'Mmmm. I'm not certain it's all been her.' Maisie smiled. 'But I have thought of something we can do to find out for sure. It does mean you'd have to put the necklace back in the jewellery box, though. But only for a little bit...'

'Arabella, I don't know what to do!' Sarah wailed. 'He's back, and he's coming to see the show tonight. He's going to take me out to supper afterwards, and I shall have to tell him I've lost the necklace. He'll hate me!'

'Maybe he won't mind,' Arabella said, clearly trying to sound hopeful.

'Not mind! It's an heirloom! It's worth thousands!' Sarah started to sob into her hands and Maisie passed her a handkerchief and a bottle of smelling salts. 'Thank you, Maisie, you're such a treasure. I really don't know what I'd do without you.' Sarah sniffed and looked up from the handkerchief. 'In fact, you should have a reward. Something nice. I know!' She seized the wooden box, and pushed it towards Maisie.

'What's that?' Arabella asked, a little sharply.

'Oh, just the box of paste jewellery from the wardrobe,' Sarah told her in a careless voice. 'I thought I'd look through it for something to brighten up my dress in the finale—it's just a little bit too dull. But I haven't had the heart, since I found out about Timmy...' She peered into the huge mirror hanging on the wall. 'Oh my goodness. I look like a hag. I look so old. Crying is the worst thing for your face, it really is. Maisie, pass me my greasepaint sticks, and then you can choose yourself something pretty out of that box. It doesn't matter what. I'll give Annie something for it, she won't mind.' Sarah drooped one eyelid in a wink as she took the greasepaint from Maisie, and then looked gloomily at her reflection. 'Ugh, dreadful.'

Maisie tried not to look at Arabella as she began to lift sparkly bracelets and rings out of the box. She mustn't let Arabella guess that this was all for her benefit. But it was so hard not to glance sideways, and see how she was taking it.

'Can I really have anything, Miss?' she murmured. 'They're all so pretty. This ring, maybe. Ooooh, or this, the green one. It's lovely.'

'Yes, any of them,' Sarah agreed, a little impatiently. 'Do you think I should go a shade darker on my cheeks, Arabella? I look so pale.'

Arabella hadn't moved a muscle. She really was a very good actress, Maisie thought.

'Then I'd like this, please, Miss,' Maisie said, drawing out the emerald pendant, and making as if to slip it back into her apron pocket.

'No!' Arabella yelped, snatching it out of her hand. And then she gasped, as Sarah and Maisie both swung round to stare at her.

'Give me that, please,' Sarah said, her voice so cold it made goosebumps rise up on Maisie's arms.

'Why—I mean—I just don't think Annie would be very happy about this going—it's a pretty piece, that's all.

She'd better choose something else,'
Arabella stuttered.

'It is pretty, isn't it?' Sarah said,
taking the necklace, and motioning to
Maisie to fasten it round her neck. 'It's
also mine. But you knew that, didn't
you.'

'I don't know what you mean...'
Arabella opened her eyes widely,
fluttering her eyelashes a little. She

looked so amazingly innocent that, for a moment, Maisie even wondered if she'd got it all wrong.

'You stole it. You could have crept in here just before the last number—you had time.' Sarah's eyes filled with tears. 'But why? Why would you have done that? I thought you were my friend!'

'Friend?' Arabella hissed, and Maisie felt a chill run down her spine as she saw the horrible look on her face. 'Why would I be your friend? You have all the luck! Dragged out of the chorus to be a star, and then your rich little lord turns up, showering you in jewels! And you're so stupid you didn't even know what it was he'd given you! Couldn't you see it was real?'

'How did you know?' Maisie asked quietly.

'My grandfather runs a little jewellery shop,' Arabella said bitterly. 'Oh, he'd never have anything like that. But I can tell a real stone when I see one. And I couldn't miss that one. Besides, I knew the stories about it. My grandfather used to tell me about all the famous jewels.'

'So you took it,' Sarah said.

'Yes. But you'll never prove it!' Arabella cried. 'Everyone knows you're always making a fuss. They won't believe you.'

Sarah gave her a strange sort of smile, and stood up, walking over to the screen in the corner, where she changed. She moved it back, so that the theatre manager could step out, and then she smiled at Arabella.

'Oh, I really think they will.'

'I can't do it!' Maisie whispered, her eyes wide with panic.

'Of course you can! It's nothing! You did far more acting in that little scene where we tricked Arabella than you need to now. Besides, Maisie, you have to. With Arabella gone, we need another girl. All you have to do is sit there and pretend to sew.' Sarah nudged her. 'And don't try to trip me up!'

'I suppose so,' Maisie muttered. 'Oh my goodness, it's starting!'

'Go on! Just follow the others, and sit down on that hay bale!' Sarah gave her a little push, and Maisie hurried out on to the stage, desperately trying not to look at the audience. She knew that if she saw that many people staring at her, she might faint.

Afterwards, she could hardly remember anything of the dance number. It seemed to fly by, and then

one of the other girls was grabbing her wrist and hauling her off with the rest.

'You see! It was fine!' Sarah hissed in her ear. 'Now you'd better get back down to the dressing room. I need to change in a minute.'

Maisie helped Sarah with her changes, like she always did for the rest of the show. But in between she sat in the corner of the dressing room, with Eddie on her lap, trying not to remember the lights, and the music, and all those people. She had never been so scared, never.

'Maisie, come on!' One of the chorus girls dived into the room. 'Oh, good, you've still got the dress on. It's the curtain call.'

'But I don't have to do that, do I?' Maisie squeaked.

'Sarah says you do. Come on!' She dragged Maisie up the stairs and actually pushed her on to the stage. The chorus girls danced on in a train, and the girl in front grabbed Maisie's hands. 'Hold me round the middle. Just skip!' And then she danced on to the stage, smiling and skipping, and Maisie had to follow her.

The audience were shouting and clapping, and throwing flowers as Sarah and the other stars bowed and bowed. Maisie wasn't surprised. Sarah must have been at her best tonight— she had been so happy, and she was about to see her fiancé. The huge emerald glowed against her throat, making her look more beautiful than ever.

One of the chorus girls gathered up the flowers and passed them to Sarah, but then she turned, and beckoned to Maisie. The two girls either side pushed her forward, and Sarah filled her arms with flowers, while Maisie blinked nervously at the sea of cheering faces.

Afterwards, in the dressing room, she frowned at Sarah. 'What are you going to tell Lord Tarquin? He's bound to ask you why you gave all your flowers to a girl in the chorus.'

Sarah smiled at her in the mirror as she wiped away her make-up. 'I'm going to tell him the truth. And then I

shall give him the necklace back. If he still wants to marry me, even when he knows I lost it, I shall ask him to give me something else. A nice little diamond, perhaps. Something *small*. Something that won't curse me if I happen to lose it!'

'Won't you miss it?' Alice asked Maisie the next day. She had convinced Miss Sidebotham that she'd left her French grammar book behind at Albion Street. 'It must have been such fun being in the theatre.'

Maisie shook her head thoughtfully. 'I don't think so. It was nice for a change, but it was ever so tiring. I don't mean the being-up-late, I mean the people. Always crying, or fighting, or having hysterical fits. I like sensible people,' she added, scratching Eddie behind the ears.

'I suppose that's what actors are like,' Alice said, nodding.

'Mmmm. Well, it's good to be back home, without anything more dramatic than Sally breaking the china,' said Maisie. 'Miss Sarah's dresser, Lucy, is a lot better now, she can hobble around. So Miss Sarah doesn't need me any more.'

'I wish you'd stayed just one more day, so you could find out what Lord Tarquin said,' Alice sighed. 'I do hope they're still getting married, it's such a lovely story.I suppose Miss Lane will tell you, though.'

'Maisie! There's someone here for you!' Gran was calling up the stairs.

Maisie jumped up. 'Who can that be?' she murmured, hurrying down.

Alice peered curiously over the banisters after her.

'Miss Maisie Hitchins?' asked the man at the door, and Maisie nodded mutely. He was extremely grand, in a black livery absolutely covered in gold braid, and there was a carriage drawn up in the street, with a crest painted on the door.

'Lord Tarquin Fane presents his compliments and asks you to accept

this small token of his gratitude,' the
man went on, holding out a jewellery
box.

Maisie took it, her hands shaking,
and the man stalked back to the
carriage.

'Whatever is it?' Gran demanded,
staring at the box. 'Open it, Maisie!'

Maisie undid the little golden hook with trembling fingers. Inside the box, on a bed of dark velvet, was a little pearl bracelet, and underneath, there was a dog collar. The smartest collar that Maisie had ever seen—dark green leather, with a buckle that sparkled in the winter sunlight shining through the open door.

'Good gracious me, Maisie, the man's sent you a diamond dog collar!' Gran cried, and Maisie began to laugh.

'It's a reward,' Maisie murmured. 'Like a real detective. People are always giving Gilbert Carrington things. But I'd much rather have a collar for Eddie than a silver-plated walking stick.'

'And the bracelet's beautiful.' Gran held it up admiringly.

Maisie nodded. 'Mm-hm.' She smiled as she fastened the sparkly collar round Eddie's neck and then put on her bracelet. She held out her hand, admiring the glow of the pearls round her wrist. They might have to keep the jewels for best, she thought. What if they went missing, like Miss Sarah's necklace?

Still, she could hang them up on her wall for the rest of the time. Perhaps Professor Tobin would lend her one of his little glass cases. They'd remind her of the glittering, dangerous world of the theatre—and the case of the vanishing emerald.